Basho and the River Stones

by *Tim Myers*

illustrations by *Oki S. Han*

Marshall Cavendish
New York ◆ London ◆ Singapore

To Matsuo Basho, in gratitude for the richness his life and work have brought
to mine; to my rich-hearted wife, who led us in raising our glasses to him;
and to Cassie, whose gift to me was the title!
—T. M.

To my friends, for their constant belief in me and my art
—O.S.H.

A *haiku* is a short poem of three lines and seventeen syllables. *Haiku* was invented in Japan and perfected by the great poet Basho. It's still very popular, both in Japan and around the world.

Text copyright © 2004 by Tim Myers
Illustrations copyright © 2004 by Oki S. Han

All rights reserved
Marshall Cavendish, 99 White Plains Road, Tarrytown, NY 10591
www.marshallcavendish.com
Library of Congress Cataloging-in-Publication Data

Myers, Tim (Tim Brian)
Basho and the river stones / by Tim Myers ; illustrations by Oki S. Han.— 1st ed.
p. cm.
Summary: Tricked by a fox into giving up his share of cherries, a famous Japanese poet is inspired to write
a haiku and the fox, ashamed of his actions, must devise another trick to set things right.
ISBN 0–7614–5165–X
1. Matsuo, Basho, 1644-1694—Juvenile fiction. [1. Matsuo, Basho, 1644–1694—Fiction. 2. Foxes—Fiction.
3. Poetry—Fiction. 4. Japan—History—17th century—Fiction.] I. Han, Oki S., ill. II. Title.

PZ7.M57195Bas 2004
E]—dc22
2003026245

The text of this book is set in Meridien Medium.
The illustrations are rendered in watercolor.
Book design by Adam Mietlowski
Printed in China
First edition
1 3 5 6 4 2

Matsuo Basho is Japan's most famous poet. But few people know how he came to be a lifelong friend to the foxes of Fukagawa.

When he first came to live near the Fuka River, Basho discovered a cherry tree on his property and agreed to share its cherries with the local foxes.

For a long time things were peaceful; between Basho and the fox clan there was great *wa*, or harmony.

But then some of the clan grew impatient and greedy. And one young fox, particularly fond of cherries, decided to play a trick on the poet.

Japanese foxes have great magic; they're especially good at transforming things—and themselves. So the young fox made himself look like a *yamabushi*, a wandering monk . . .

and picked three stones out of the river.

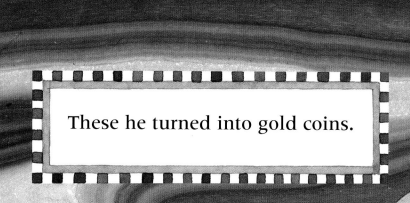

These he turned into gold coins.

The fox knew Basho was poor. So when he approached the poet's bare little hut and saw Basho reading in the sunshine, he said, in his best monk-voice, "A good-hearted merchant gave me these coins, and I want to do a kindness with them in return. I've noticed that the foxes around here look very hungry. If I give you these coins, will you sign a paper saying you'll leave the cherries of that beautiful tree only for them?"

Basho was quite hungry himself. He had little money for food since he spent his time writing and wandering in the woods and fields. And cherries, though delicious, only come once a year. So he agreed, setting the coins carefully on a low table in his hut. Then he picked up his calligraphy brush and wrote what the fox-monk had suggested, signing it with his name.

At that the monk went on his way, chuckling to himself.

The next day the young fox couldn't wait to sneak up to the hut; he wanted to see how angry Basho would be once the magic wore off and the coins turned back into stones.

But when he peeked in at the window, he saw Basho writing, with a huge smile on his face and the three river stones on the table before him. The fox was confused. Suddenly Basho noticed the fox's ears sticking up above the window ledge.

"Ah, *kitsune*!" Basho called happily, "come see what good fortune I've had!" The curious fox trotted around the hut and came in through the door.

"Yesterday a monk visited me," Basho began, "and paid me three gold coins to leave all the cherries for you foxes. But some fox must have tricked that monk—because they weren't really coins at all. This morning they turned back into river stones. But see how beautiful they are!" The poet held up one of the water-rounded stones, admiring its smooth surface and rich color.

"At first I was angry and disappointed to lose the gold," Basho continued. "How foolish that was! Suddenly, as I looked carefully at the stones, I understood—and a poem came to me!"

How many years have
these stones loved the river, not
knowing they were poor?

When he heard this, the young fox was amazed. And suddenly he felt ashamed.

"Master!" the fox said sorrowfully, "forgive me! I'm the one who tricked you, pretending to be a monk. I was blind and selfish—but you understood what was really important! I should have remembered that many things are more valuable than gold!"

Basho looked surprised, but then he nodded. "A good poem is worth more than money—and it lasts much longer," he said. "Thank you for being honest with me, *kitsune*."

"And thank you for teaching me," the fox said. Then he bowed low and left.

The fox returned to his lair with a heavy heart. Sitting alone, he wondered how he could ever repay the debt of gratitude he now owed Basho.

Then it came to him—the three *riyo* he'd buried beneath the stone lantern at the temple of Inari! Those gold coins—real ones—could buy the poet enough food for the whole winter.

The fox dug them up and returned to Basho's hut.

"Master," he said seriously, "you must let me tear up that paper you signed, giving us foxes all the cherries. I was dishonest with you; it shouldn't count!"

But Basho wouldn't hear of it, as the fox had expected. "I'm afraid I can't let you do that," Basho said. "I accept your kind apology, but I've already signed the paper. It would be dishonorable to pretend I hadn't."

"Then at least let me pay you for the cherries!" the fox pleaded, showing Basho the coins and assuring him they were real.

"Ah, *kitsune*—I don't mean to be difficult. But you already paid me for the cherries. The river stones you gave were beautiful, and they helped me find a poem; that was more than enough! My honor won't allow me to accept charity."

Again the fox left feeling guilty and perplexed.

Slowly he made his way through the woods to the banks of the Fuka River, pausing there with his head hung in shame. But he happened to glance at the purling water and noticed, just beneath its surface, more beautiful river stones. Suddenly he lifted his head and smiled. *Now I know what to do!* he told himself.

The next day he returned to Basho's hut, carrying a small bag. Basho frowned when he saw the fox approaching. Would the creature try to give him the coins again?

"Master," the fox said, bowing deeply, "I thought about what you said—and I understand. So today I've come, not with charity, but with a small gift to show my appreciation." At that the fox turned the little bag upside down. Out tumbled three beautiful river stones.

Basho's face broke into a glowing smile. "Ah, *kitsune*!" he said. "What a perfect gift! Yes, I accept them— perhaps they'll inspire another poem. Thank you. You are too kind!"

The fox could hardly contain his happiness; but then he said, hesitating a little, "So . . . you promise to keep my gift?"

"Of course," Basho answered, reaching down to stroke the fox's head.

"Oh, Master!" the fox exclaimed, "I am so pleased!" With that he scampered off.

That night, before Basho went to his sleeping mat, he looked at the three new stones where he'd set them on his table. Then he smiled to himself and blew out the candle.

When he woke with the sun the next morning, he sat up and stretched—but suddenly stopped. For there on the table—just where he'd left the river stones—were three gold coins, glinting in the light from the window!

Basho hurriedly went to the table, picking up each of the coins and feeling it. They were real—he was sure of it.

あなたとともに
食べた チェリーが
一番おいしかった。

Looking closer, he realized they were the same coins
the fox had tried to give him before!

Suddenly he understood—and burst out laughing.
They hadn't been river stones at all! The magical fox had
tricked him again!

What a clever kitsune! the poet said to himself—*for he
knows I must keep a promise—even one he tricked me into making.*
So Basho picked up the coins and said a quick prayer of
gratitude, knowing he could now buy food for the winter.

Thinking the fox might be watching from somewhere,
he went to the door and stepped outside to call him in.
But all he saw was a paper fastened to the wall of the hut.

Dear Master:

*Thank you again for promising to keep the gift! And just
as the first river stones inspired you to write a haiku, these have
inspired me . . .*

I've eaten cherries alone—
but they're much sweeter
when shared with a friend.

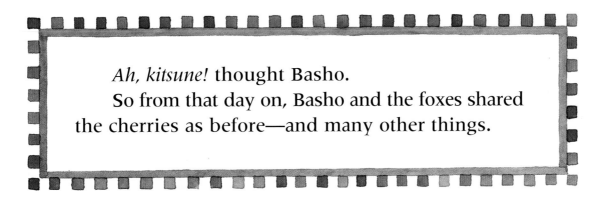

Ah, kitsune! thought Basho.

So from that day on, Basho and the foxes shared the cherries as before—and many other things.

Author's Note

Though he was born four hundred years ago, Matsuo Basho is still Japan's most revered poet. He lived a life of simplicity, spirituality, and endless travel, all of which found expression in his writing. More than anyone else, he was responsible for making the short poem called *haiku* into the deep and beautiful art form it is today.

Basho dedicated his life to seeing, smelling, tasting, feeling, hearing, considering, and appreciating in the most intense way possible, with his whole being. The power of haiku poetry begins in paying this kind of attention to the world and all that's in it, the strong and the weak, the large and the small, the dramatic and the often-overlooked. Basho teaches us that true understanding begins when we take nothing for granted. I wanted this story to echo that idea.

My daughter, Cassie, suggested the title—and it took me a while to realize that emphasizing the river stones was exactly right. (I wrote the story, but she was thinking like Basho while I played the ignorant fox!) Even Basho doesn't "see" the river stones at first, caught up as he is in other concerns—but then he understands the true preciousness of what's come to him, as does the fox in his turn. And it's not only the particular beauties of the world, such as river stones, that we're sometimes blind to, but also the radiance of life itself.

I should add that, though it includes elements from folklore, this story is my own, including the two *haiku*. I offer them joyfully and humbly in Basho's memory. For I too owe him an *ongaeshi*, a debt of gratitude, which I feel I can never fully repay.

—Tim Myers

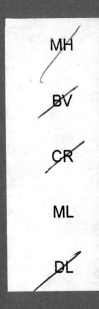